PAPERBACK EDITION

A BESTIARY ALPHABET © 2019 Mirror World Publishing and Felix Eddy

Illustrations © 2019 Felix Eddy

Edited by Robert Dowsett

All Rights Reserved. Published March 1st, 2020

Mirror World Publishing
Windsor, Ontario
www.mirrorworldpublishing.com
info@mirrorworldpublishing.com
Mirror World Publishing publications data available upon request

ISBN: 978-1-987976-66-3

I dedicate this book to my two best friends:

Deanna who supported me through a rough time and helped research all of these creatures while we sat in tents at dozens of art festivals.

And David, whose love & creativity has inspired many more projects- I look forward to a lifetime of collaboration with you.

A Bestiary Alphabet

By Felix Eddy

About this Book

This book is a compilation of drawings that stemmed from my personal fascination with mythological creatures. When I started this project, I wanted to draw my own vision of a historical mythical creature for every letter of the alphabet. The choices were simple—I chose the subjects based on which ones sounded like the most fun to draw! Finding animals for every letter was actually easier than I expected. Some creatures I was familiar with from reading fairy tales, fantasy books, watching movies, and my lifetime of "research" on the subject (funny how when you like something you just find out everything you can about it without ever thinking that you are doing "research"). Some of the beasties in this compilation feel to me like old friends. I have known them and had images of them in my mind and sketchbooks since I was eight years old. Some creatures I discovered for the very first time while working on this book.

I am frequently asked how long a drawing takes to complete. The answer is "I really don't know". I don't think about time when I draw, and I have never bothered to set a timer. Often I work on a drawing for a few minutes here and there until it's done. Many of the creatures in this book were conceived and completed during lunch breaks at work. Some took many lunch breaks, and others took only one or two. The process began with drawings in pencil in a sketchbook that I carried around with me. Later, I fleshed out the pencils with fine-point permanent marker. All of the drawings are freehand, with certain digital elements for the borders. If I had to guess, I would estimate that I spent two or three hours on average per drawing.

One thing I discovered during the research process is that there is a rich diversity of magical beasts across all cultures and in every religion. Human beings have been inventing supernatural creatures since the existence of language. Some beasts can be traced to misinterpreted descriptions of real animals, but for every one of these misrepresentations of nature there are dozens of purely magical inventions. Before we installed streetlights on every corner and huddled safe in our well-lit houses, looking into the darkness beyond the hearth fire inspired people to imagine monsters of all varieties. To this day, children everywhere spontaneously invent terrible and horrifying beasts that live under their beds, in their closets, and under the basement stairs. Fewer adults today are familiar with that nameless dread we feel when we huddle in the dark around a tiny campfire in the woods or the titillating and spooky certainty of being watched by unnatural eyes in the dark. When we "grow up" we are expected to leave our childhood fears—and our imaginary friends—behind. Adults aren't supposed to allow that creeping dread to make them dash past the dark corner of the basement, but some of us still get a little thrill out of the idea of supernatural manifestations following us around. The proliferation of "ghost hunting" TV shows and the perpetual outpouring of vampire and werewolf novels, television shows, and movies are perfect examples of our ongoing fascination with these creatures. They capture our imaginations and make us dream...sometimes they even make us scream.

But mythological creatures are more than just fantasy and make-believe. They symbolize something much deeper, more primal—all of the magic and wonder that gets lost in the regular shuffle of our lives. They also symbolize the world's dangerous and chaotic forces that offer magical riches one instant and in the next can make us fear for our lives.

I know much about mythical animals because I am in love with mythology, fables, and legends. However, this collection is by no means a comprehensive resource for mythical animals. It does not represent every creature ever imagined, and I don't make any pretense of covering every culture or having in-depth written research about each creature. There are thousands of creatures that didn't make it into this book, not because they didn't deserve the attention, but because there are only so many letters in the alphabet!

THE BESTIARY

A bestiary is a written compendium of creatures, plants, and occasionally rocks and minerals, usually heavily illustrated and decorated. Bestiary books were popular in the Middle Ages, especially in France and England, but have probably existed in some form ever since the first written stories. The earliest known bestiary book was dated to 2nd century Greece.

In Europe between the 5th and 16th centuries, bestiaries contained not just invented animals but real ones, along with fables related to the supposed qualities and metaphorical significance of each creature depicted. Not unlike Aesop's Fables, medieval bestiary stories almost always came with a moral message. Many of the anecdotes in these books would link animals to biblical stories and show parallels between nature and religion. In the Middle Ages, early Christian scholars relied heavily on religious beliefs to inform their scientific study. It was widely accepted that God created each animal, plant, and mineral, with a specific purpose in His plan. Bestiaries not only compiled and catalogued wild beasts, but they also illustrated the lessons to be learned from each example.

Medieval man did not travel as much as we do today. Travel was perilous and time consuming, and as most people were farmers, they were tied to their land and farms. Many folks kept to their plots of land for generations, often living their entire lives in one locale. Stories of the world beyond would come from a few travelers, merchants, soldiers, and bards, and the very occasional written books these travelers brought with them. Sometimes the fanciful bestiaries were the only reference that people in medieval Europe had for the creatures beyond their immediate area. Elephants, camels, and alligators certainly sounded like supernatural monsters to the average medieval European. Contrary to modern notions about medieval people being uneducated, many people in the Middle Ages actually knew how to read, and books like a bestiary would provide great storytelling entertainment for people from many walks of life.

Many of the most fanciful monsters described in the medieval bestiaries can be traced to real live animals. Some accounts of unicorns have been traced to misinterpreted descriptions of rhinoceros or certain deer. Some bizarre creatures probably grew from the misunderstanding of translated names of real beasts from one country to another. Some regular animals were attributed supernatural qualities because their nature wasn't fully understood. The mythical salamanders that were supposed to be born out of fire were based on the real live salamanders that were drawn to the warm earth near a fire pit. Certain animals in bestiaries were known not to exist at all, but were allegories for certain alchemical processes. Some had been passed down through the centuries as factual creatures. The ancient Greeks categorized dozens of animals in volumes of writing—as natural beasts, separate from mythology—including unicorns.

THE AL-MI'RAJ

The al-mi'raj is a Middle Eastern beast that looks like a very large yellow rabbit with a long black horn growing from its head. Sometimes called simply a-mi'raj, they are said to kill and eat horses, and are very deadly to humans. They are featured in Islamic poetry and said to live on a mysterious island somewhere in the Indian Ocean.

Highly skilled traveling witches were the only ones able to destroy these creatures and prevent them from returning to an area. In fact, it's likely that these "highly skilled traveling witches" actually spread rumors of these creatures so they could use their "skills" to exterminate them— for a price. They didn't have to stretch the truth too far, though, because the al-mi'raj was possibly based on real life "attack bunnies".

There are a few diseases that afflict rabbits, causing lumpy growths or making their fur matt up painfully, appearing like horns, or like bumps where a horn fell off. These rabbits are often driven mad with pain from their twisted and matted fur, which can make them unusually aggressive. While it's doubtful that a rabbit could kill a horse, even if it was mad with pain, certainly a rabbit that was acting insane and rushing at people would cause some real alarm— perhaps enough to start the myth of a monstrous horned rabbit.

Horned rabbits have been translated into modern use by a number of fantasy writers and game companies. They are featured in video games and role-playing game books, both as monsters and as humorous creatures, called "horned rabbits" or "bunnycorns" or "unibunnies".

Al Mí'raj

THE BASILISK

A basilisk is said to emerge from an egg laid by a *rooster* that is incubated by a lizard or toad. The basilisk and the Cockatrice are very closely related in their legendary origins (although a cockatrice is supposed to have hatched from an egg laid by a lizard and hatched by the rooster). Often, the two words are used interchangeably to speak of the same animal. Certainly, all depictions of the mythical beasts have the appearance of a rooster and a snake or lizard mixed up together somehow. Sometimes the basilisk is depicted more lizard-like and without wings, or as a lizard creature with a chicken's head and six lizard legs. Each of these creatures can turn you to stone with a look, and sometimes they are reputed to be able to wither plants with their breath.

Tales of the basilisk have been around since biblical times. In the Bible, Isaiah 14:29 has a basilisk as the parent of fiery serpents. References to these creatures have appeared in Chaucer's *Canterbury Tales*, Shakespeare's *Richard III*, and, in more modern times, in contemporary poetry and novels like *Harry Potter*.

The curious method of its birth and magical properties made the basilisk a useful symbol in Alchemy in the Middle Ages. Alchemy is a combination of science and magic with the primary focus of turning common metals to gold, but was also concerned with the purification of the human soul. "basilisk blood" was featured in several formulas, and the basilisk was often used to represent the destructive force of fire.

Basilisk

THE CENTAUR

Centaurs are half-man, half-horse creatures that featured prominently in Greek mythology. Centaurs were considered lusty, wild, and fierce. They were dangerous, easily intoxicated, and mostly feral. However, one or two of them seemed to be able to overcome their wild nature to become civilized and honorable creatures. The centaur Chiron was noted for his honor and wisdom, and was cited as having tutored several notable Greek youths, including Achilles, Jason, and Asclepius. Chiron was well versed in surgery, magic, and herbal lore, and taught his young apprentices all that he knew, helping them to become legendary heroes.

Symbolically, centaurs embody the duality of human nature. They represent the parts of our psyche at war with our intellectual mind. The noble centaurs of legend demonstrate how we can choose to overcome our base instincts and become intellectual creatures, while their feral brethren show us the consequences of living only to feed our baser instincts. The noble and enlightened centaur has become a popular feature of many modern fantasy novels and stories, even appearing in television shows and movies.

There is some speculation that the origins of the centaur may have actually come from the first interaction of one early horse-less culture with mounted nomads. The horseback riders may well have appeared to be half-beast to people unfamiliar with horses, and certainly nomadic tribes were very fierce. A similar misconception was reported of the Aztecs by the Spanish conquistadors when they first encountered mounted cavalry.

Centaur

THE DJINN

Djinn, also known as jinn, or genies, are powerful creatures that exist in a parallel world to our own and possess strong magical powers. Djinn are mentioned in the Koran as one of the three beings created by Allah with free will. They are more magical and powerful than humans, but lesser beings than the Angels.

Some theories hold that the djinn are demons, and that Satan was one of the most powerful djinn who disobeyed God. Because they have free will, djinn can be good or evil, and follow any religion they choose. There are different kinds of djinn, who control different kinds of elemental forces. The Ifreet, for example, control fire, and are often depicted as winged beings made all or partly out of flames. The djinn come from another plane of existence, but live much like humans, with governments and laws, marriages and families. Sometimes they can be tricked or trapped by humans and made to serve a human master.

King Solomon is said to have trapped all the djinn in enchanted bottles to keep them from destroying our world. These enchanted djinn must grant three wishes to the human who frees them, sometimes the story goes that the third wish must always be used to put the jinn back into the bottle, or the freed creature will destroy their one-time master!

Djinn

THE ENFIELD

The enfield is a Heraldic beast, which means that it was basically assembled to adorn crests and shields— specifically for the O'Kelly family of Ireland. It is described as having the head of a fox, the chest of a greyhound, the body of a lion, the hindquarters and tail of a wolf, and forelegs like an eagle's talons. There is only one recorded anecdotal instance of the creature beyond its appearance on shield and crests, when it emerged from the sea to protect the body of the fallen chieftain Tadhg Mor O'Kelly, so that he could be properly retrieved and buried by his brethren.

While the enfield is fairly obscure even in the realm of mythical beings, there persist to this day enfield enthusiasts who will argue over whether the beast originated with the O'Kelly family or in Enfield, Middlesex, and whether it has the chest of an elephant or a greyhound! The combination of animals on a heraldic crest has subtly different connotations, but mainly the fox head designates cunning and intelligence, the various animals suggested for the body represent its strength and fierceness, and the eagle's talons are suggestive of its power, honor, and nobility. My version of the enfield has him looking a bit foxier and sporting wings. Adding wings, crowns, or talons to various creatures is a longstanding tradition in heraldry, often used to designate offshoots of a house or to place a family in a certain region. I felt my enfield needed to look a bit craftier. Scotland, Ireland and Britain are rife with tales of the fae folk (fairies), and it's likely that the enfield is related to other fae creatures—making his sly look all the more appropriate.

Enfield

THE FAUN

Fauns are goat-like people with horns and hooves, found in Roman mythology. They are associated with nature spirits, and often connected to a certain glen or woodland. Physically, fauns are similar to Satyrs, the goat-like men that were renowned in Greek mythology for their wild, lusty ways and their following of the Greek god of wine, Dionysus. Satyrs, unlike fauns, were supposed to have human feet, and were wilder and uncontrollable, sometimes described simply as "wild men" with a few bestial attributes. Fauns, by comparison, are relatively gentle creatures who guard wild nature and protect agricultural herds from wolves. They are often associated with the Roman god Faunus and goddess Fauna, who are also depicted as goat-people.

The similarity between the Faunus of Roman mythology and Cernnunos, the nature god of Celtic mythology, is interesting to note. Cernnunos was also depicted as a hairy, antlered man who defended nature and was a guardian of wild animals. Both of these ancient deities can be considered archetypes of male forces. Wild, powerful, hairy and fierce, they epitomize a lot of masculine attributes. They have both recently been re-imagined as the modern Pagan "Horned God," who represents the sun and masculine powers. Loosely based on these ancient deities, the Horned God is often represented by a man with antlers or horns, and the faun and satyr have experienced a resurgence of popularity with the followers of these nature based religions.

In modern culture, the faun was rediscovered by writer C.S. Lewis in his beloved *Chronicles of Narnia*. The faun, Mr. Tumnus, was a shy character who assisted the heroes of the story. A number of recent authors have worked the faun into their stories, bringing these creatures back into movies and books.

Faun

THE GRIFFIN

The gryphon (or more conventionally spelled "griffin") has been circulating in lore in Mesopotamia and Egypt since 3300 BC. Usually, the griffin is described as having the head and forelegs of an eagle, and the body of a lion, sometimes having lion-like or feathered ears. griffins were thought to be the offspring of the Eagle (considered the "King of the Birds") and the Lion ("King of the Beasts"). Based on their noble lineage, griffins were much revered, as they were thought to embody the best traits of each creature.

Like dragons and many other mythical beasts, griffins were believed to guard treasures, and to defend their hordes with extreme ferocity. They were also said to mate for life, and if one half of a mated pair passed away, the other would spend the rest of its days alone—a belief that caused the Catholic Church to use a griffin as a symbol of its' views on re-marriage. Strangely, from the griffin we also get hippogriffs, which were supposed to be the result of the union of a griffin and a mare (usually the griffin's favorite prey). A hippogriff has the head and talons of an eagle, and the body of a horse.

Because of its regal lineage, and the nobility of the Lion and the Eagle, the griffin was often used in heraldry for royalty. It was also often used in Catholic symbolism as a representation of Christ. Because of the union of the earthbound lion and the mighty flying eagle, the church drew parallels between the joining of man and God in the creation of Jesus. This lead to the popularity of griffin sculptures on churches, and the often reoccurring images of griffins in the sculptures and gargoyles on Catholic churches.

Griffin

THE HARPY

Harpies have alternately been described as hideous and foul or beautiful and fair. It seems that originally harpies were wind goddesses, or personifications of storm winds, and later were confused or combined with Greek Sirens, who were also described as bird-women but were undeniably evil, luring sailors to their deaths. The word that "harpy" is derived from means literally "to snatch", which was suitable for their first incarnation as wind goddesses, as well as their later depiction as grabby, vicious monsters.

Harpies sometimes appear in threes, like the Furies, Gorgons, and Fates in Greek legends. They tormented many a famous mythical hero, stealing food from plates and decimating herds of cattle and sheep. Harpies seem to be the embodiment of greed—they have insatiable appetites and are perpetually eating.

The harpies sometimes acted as emissaries to the Furies, or messengers of the Underworld. They might be sent to collect someone for torment, or to drag evildoers to Hades. Among the terrible progeny of the Echidna (the Mother of All Monsters) and Typhon (a beast with a hundred heads) the harpies are almost always malevolent, and often considered insane. Their appearance and combination of beautiful human faces and hideous and unclean vulture-like bodies seems to physically manifest their madness.

Harpy

THE ICTHYOCENTAUR

In Greek mythology, there were a pair of sea-gods, Aphros and Bythos (who were also, coincidentally, half-brothers of the wise centaur Chiron) described as having the upper bodies of men, the legs of horses, and the tails of fish, sometimes lobster claw horns on their heads. They were depicted in a number of ancient mosaics, and the mixture of men, horses and sea creatures may have been influenced by the cult of Posiedon, who was the god of both horses and the seas. Several sculptural and artistic representations of these unusual beasts, known as ichthyocentaurs (fish-centaurs), feature lion-like forelegs, rather than horse legs. Sometimes they are considered sons of Triton, other times they are called "Tritons", like part of a race of these mermen and mer-creatures. Often, these unusual sea creatures are depicted as heralds or emissaries of Triton, a god of the sea.

Ichthyocentaurs are relatively obscure monsters, possibly derived as a centaur-like relative of the sea-horse hippocamps, which are half-horse and half-fish and found in Greek, Etruscan, and Phoenician mythology. Ichthyocentaurs primarily feature in artwork relating to other sea-gods and sea-monster legends, as though they are secondary characters, playing only support roles. It's possible that they arose out of some confusion or re-interpretation of the Syrian legend of the divine fish that carried Astarte ashore after her birth in the sea. These divine fish were later set in the stars as the constellation Pisces.

Icthyocentaur

THE JACULUS

The jaculus is a small winged serpent, or diminutive winged dragon, that appeared often in medieval bestiaries. The jaculus sometimes appears as a snake with wings, or occasionally with front legs and wings. The beast would hide in trees, launching itself at victims like a javelin, giving it the nickname the javelin snake.

The jaculus bears many resemblances to venomous fandrefiala snakes in Madagascar, which launch themselves from trees to spear their prey, and will attack humans and animals alike. The jaculus, however, is purported to fly after its victims, and is also quite formidable on the ground. The jaculus was not thought to be venomous, it killed with the force of its bite, rather than poison. It may have been based on a real snake that jumped on its prey from the trees, although whether the source of the legend was the fandrefiala snake, or something else isn't clear.

The jaculus was first documented Pliny the Edler, who also documented the unicorn, and also Lucan, who described a jaculus attack in particularly gruesome terms. There is also a reference to a jaculus in the Old Norse Romance, Yngvars saga viðfǫrla, though in that instance it was supposed to be a very large and dangerous dragon.

Jaculus

THE KRAKEN

The kraken is an enormous sea monster that originated in Scandinavian legends. Originally, kraken were described as being so large that they looked like small islands, sometimes with trees on their backs. They could drag an entire ship under the waves with them, or sometimes the giant whirlpool vortex left behind them when they submerged would pull down whole fleets of ships.

Early accounts of the kraken had them as more crab-like monsters with a shell, but eventually they came to be known as giant octopus or squid monsters. Norway and Scandinavia, where the legends originated, are very dependent on their fishing and ocean travel, so the perils of the unknown ocean were very real to them. Giant squid have been sighted by many sailors, and there is proof now that many of these "mythical" accounts might have stemmed from real encounters with giant squid. Remains of *Architeuthis*, a species of giant squid, have been found up to 50 feet long, and purportedly have attacked ships.

The kraken and other mysterious sea monsters continue to fascinate writers, artists, and movie-makers. Something primal about the inhospitable, unknown depths of the open ocean seems to capture the human imagination like nothing else. The kraken is only one of many leviathans that lurk the oceans of legend, but the scientific evidence for the existence of the giant squid leads some to wonder what else might lurk below the surface.

kraken

THE LEOKAMPOI

The leokampoi, or sea-lion, is an Etruscan variation of a hippocamp, or sea-horse. Often featured in tomb decorations as guardians, leokampoi have the front half of a lion and the rear half of a fish or dolphin. Sometimes they appear with wings, just like their equine counterparts, the hippocamps.

Hippocamps were depicted as the steeds of Poseidon, the Greek god of the ocean and horses. The leokampoi and its relatives, pardalokampoi (leopard-fish), were more predominant in Etruscan art and mythology. Much like the Ichthyocentaur, these obscure but fantastic beasts seemed to feature most predominantly in sculpture and art to support more iconic water deities, or as supplemental decorations to bathhouses and public fountains.

The Etruscans were a significant maritime power around 500 BC, and it's no surprise that they had a lot of ocean-related imagery in their artwork and legends. Later, in the Middle Ages throughout Europe, the use of fabulous mythical beasts for heraldry became widespread. The hippocamp and the leokampoi were often used in heraldry for nobility with a strong connection to the ocean, or a strong naval presence.

Leokampoi

THE MANTICORE

Another popular feature in medieval Bestiaries, the manticore was originally a Persian monster, first noted in 4th Century BC. Said to be either from Ethiopia (like the sphinx in the tale of Oedipus) or India, manticores are described as huge red lions with the faces of men and three rows of teeth. They have either the tail of a scorpion or a tail with a fan of spines, like porcupine quills, which they can sting with at close quarters or hurl like darts at enemies. Every part of the manticore is poisonous, and it can kill a man with just one bite or scratch. With its triple rows of teeth, the manticore can consume a human bones and all, leaving no trace. Manticores are supposed to have a voice like a trumpet and pan pipes or a flute playing simultaneously.

Occasionally a manticore is depicted as having wings, or having talons like a dragon or reptile; sometimes it has horns, and sometimes it doesn't. There has been speculation (even as early as 77AD) that descriptions of the manticore are based on either lions or tigers, and have been exaggerated by indigenous people's extreme fear of the wild beasts. The legends of the manticore persisted, and they were featured in early compilations of natural history as well as bestiaries. The manticore was even featured in many medieval churches as a symbolic representation of the prophet Jeremiah (known for his doom-filled prophecies). The word "manticore" is apparently a misinterpretation of the greek word *martichoras,* which means "man-eater."

Manticore

THE NAGA

Nagas are powerful water and nature spirits with many of snake-like characteristics. Naga are sometimes depicted as serpents, as cobras with many heads, or as half-snake men (and women). In stories, the naga are often shapechangers, being human at first and then changing to more snake-like forms later.

In Tibet, naga defend nature and live in underground streams, where they guard treasures and gemstones. In India, Nepal, and Bali, nagas feature in a lot of Hindu legends, including creation stories and epic hero myths, where they may be good or evil. Often there are both good and evil nagas in the same story. Nagas are also devoted protectors of the Buddha and his teachings. The naga, Mucalinda, shields the meditating Buddha with the hoods on his seven heads to protect him from a storm. To this day, many statues depict the Buddha with a sort of umbrella of cobras over his head to commemorate this devoted naga.

There are scores of paintings and sculptures of naga all over Asia. They are most frequently depicted as beautiful women from the waist-up and snakes from the waist down, or as many-headed serpents. There is an often repeated image in Asian artwork that features a naga couple entwined from the waist down, to represent a happy marriage.

Naga

The Otso

The word "Otso" and many other names for this Finnish woodland spirit are rarely spoken aloud—and never *ever* uttered in the woods. The otso is a bear spirit, or a nature spirit that often takes to form of a bear. Some legend has it that the otso is the soul of a person (or many souls from many persons) lost in the woods. Not necessarily malevolent, the otso is fearsome and undoubtedly dangerous. It can appear as an ordinary bear or it can be unseen in the woods, consisting of scuffling noises and half-glimpsed shadows that seem to follow a traveler.

Finnish lore has a lot of references to bears, and there is a historical precedence for bear worship among the earliest people to live in Finland. Since bears were fearsome predators that could walk on two legs like men, and enjoyed all the same foods that people did—including grain, honey and salmon—the early people considered them soulful and intelligent creatures. The otso is often called "friend," "brother," or "king of the forest," rather than called by one of its proper names. The otso may help weary travelers, or punish trespassers in its territory, so it is best not to call its attention by using its proper name. In some places, to this day if a bear is killed some will put its skull in a natural clearing and leave offerings to appease the bear's spirit.

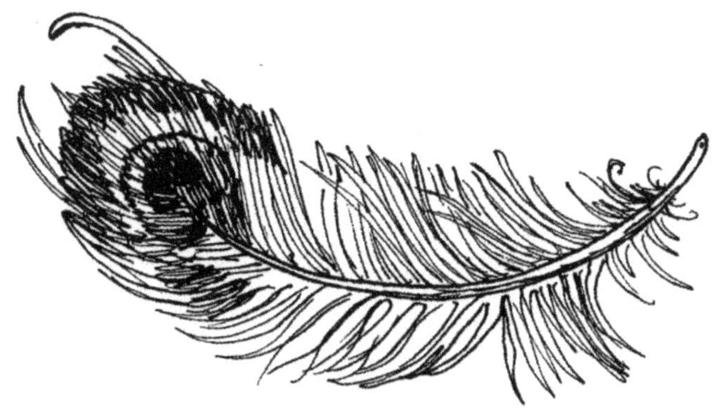

THE PHOENIX

Stories of a bird rising from fire, being made of fire, or being immortal or indestructible are common in many cultures. The very first phoenix legend probably comes from ancient Egyptian religious rites. The Egyptians had a bird called a benu, depicted as a grey heron with either two feathers in its crest or wearing the headdress of Osiris (the god who dies and is reborn). The benu was a representation of the sun, which "dies" every evening and is "reborn" the next day.

The Greeks took the Egyptian legend and embellished it, turning the tale of resurrection into an epic in which the bird lives for 500 years, creates its own funeral pyre, and is reborn from the ashes of its own father. This story provided later Christians with a perfect parallel to the resurrection of Christ, and the phoenix was adopted into Christian iconography.

In China, the phoenix is called Feng Huang. Originally two birds, a male and a female, the Feng Huang eventually joined into one being, a female bird that came to be associated with the Chinese Empress. Beside the Chinese Dragon, who is the symbol of the Emperor, the phoenix is the next most revered legendary creature in Chinese culture.

In Persia, the phoenix equivalent is a divine bird called the Simurgh. The Simurgh has the appearance of a giant peacock, sometimes with the forelegs of a lion, and indescribably beautiful plumage. Sometimes referred to as the King of Birds, the Simurgh is immortal, mystical, and can travel through time and space.

In alchemy, the phoenix is often used to represent the purifying heat of fire and generally denotes the successful completion of an alchemical experiment.

Phoenix

THE QILIN

The qilin is often described as the "Chinese Unicorn", though it may have two pronged antlers. The qilin (or Chi'l lin) is a stocky-bodied beast often depicted with scales, with a goat-like or lion-like body, a lion-like tail, a flowing mane, hooves, and often tusks. Sometimes they appear like a Chinese dragon with the body of a horse. The Japanese "Kirin" is very similar creature, but more deer-like and slender. Both the Chinese and Japanese versions of this beast are gentle and noble, do not eat meat, can move silently without disturbing a single blade of grass, and sometimes walk on water.

It is said that these creatures will only punish the wicked, and they instinctively know right from wrong. In legend, a prominent and noble judge used to rely on the ability of the qilin to determine the guilt or innocence of an accused man. The appearance of the qilin is supposed to be a good omen, and can herald the birth or coming of a great sage. The most famous legend regarding the qilin tells that the mother of the great Chinese philosopher Confucius met one of these creatures before she gave birth to her famous son. The legend continues that before his death, Confucius received word that some thoughtless hunters had killed a qilin in the woods, and he knew it was a portent of his own demise.

In 1414 the Chinese Emperor was presented with a pair of giraffes, which were called qilin and kept in the palace as honored pets. To this day, in Japan and Korea, the giraffe is called a "Kirin," but it is unlikely that giraffes had much to do with the original qilin, since they are all shown with much shorter necks. Sculptures of qilin often guard tombs and temples in China. After the dragon and the phoenix, the qilin is the next most revered legendary beast in China.

Quilin

THE RAKSHASA

The rakshasa is a race of magical people who feature prominently in a number of Hindu legends. Predominantly evil, bloodthirsty warriors or unclean spirits, it seems that the rakshasa could change shape almost at will, taking on fearsome countenances to terrify enemies on the battlefield. Sometimes described as "Hungry Ghosts," the rakshasa may scavenge the battlefield to consume the dead.

Though they seem to be able to assume any form they desire, the rakshasa seem to prefer taking on a tiger's head with monstrous tusks and a man's body. According to Hindu beliefs, many rakshasa are the reincarnated souls of especially wicked humans. They can alter their appearance, but some of this may be an illusion, and if a hero is strong and pure enough they can see through the tricks of the rakshasa.

Though they seem to be predisposed to be evil beings, there are some rakshasa that fight alongside heroes and fight for good. The legends that feature these monsters often seem to treat them as supernatural mercenaries—they like violence and the rush to fight, but they may not all be strictly evil...some are just overzealous. There is a story in Buddhist lore that involves a rakshasa that repeatedly harasses the Buddha, until finally he is swayed by the Buddhas patience and kindness to become a follower, remaining loyal to Buddha's teachings ever after.

Rakshasa

THE SPHINX

There are several variations on the basic idea of a sphinx, depending on what region the lore comes from. In India, sphinxes guard temples and sacred places. When they are stationed at the entryway of a sacred place they are said to take away the sins of those who enter and drive away evil spirits. These and other Asian sphinxes can be male or female, generally have the body of a lion (sometimes with wings), and often wear ornamental jewelry and headdresses.

Egyptian sphinxes could be either a lioness with a woman's head or a lion with the head of a pharaoh or a man. These sphinxes frequently acted as temple guardians as well. Generally associated with the feline solar deities Bast and Sehkmet, sometimes the Egyptian sphinxes could stand in as guardians for different gods when they featured different animal heads. The Greek historian, Heredotus, when writing about the Egyptian sphinxes, called the ram-headed sphinxes, criosphinxes, and the bird-headed ones, heirocosphinxes. The human headed ones were known as androsphinxes.

The Greeks were extremely enamored with Egyptian sphinxes, and they adapted a version of the creatures for their own legends. The word "sphinx" is from the greek word which means "strangler" or "to strangle." In Greek mythology there is only one sphinx, and she is a daughter of Echidna and Typhon (like the harpies and a lot of other Greek monsters). The Greek sphinx is a harbinger of bad luck, and she was set to guard the entrance to the Greek city of Thebes. There she asked travelers a riddle to pass through the gates, and she tore to bits the unlucky ones who couldn't answer her.

Later, during the 16th century, French sculptors seemed to rediscover the sphinx and re-imagined her as a coiffed and decorated guardian. In the 1800's the Symbolist painters again revived the image of the sphinx, this time as a representation of the creative forces that drive an artist to make work. According to the Symbolists, the seductive beauty of the sphinx was what inspired an artist, while the deadly, monstrous claws were representative of the self-destructive drive of an unsuccessful or unproductive artist.

Sphinx

THE TIANLONG

The tianlong is literally the "Heavenly Dragon" in Chinese legend. The most revered and holy of creatures in Chinese mythology, the Heavenly Dragon is a flying dragon associated with water and weather. The tianlong is considered a good omen and good luck. The heavenly dragon has long been a symbol of the masculine element (*yang*) especially when paired with the Chinese phoenix who represents the feminine element (*yin*).

tianlong are revered as good and noble creatures, if somewhat capricious. Their appearance in support of an emperor was evidence of auspicious times. They were said to guard the celestial home of the gods, and sometimes served to pull the chariots of the gods. There is significance to the number of claws that a celestial dragon is pictured as having as well: the five-clawed tianlong were generally assigned to emperors, while four-clawed relatives were for nobility, and three-clawed dragons were associated with commoners.

Generally, the Chinese dragon is depicted as a long, scaly serpent with a colorful ridge of scales on its back and a horse-like head with a mane. The tianlong usually has antlered horns like a deer, and large, tusk-like teeth. The dragon is often found in decorations and sculptures for good luck all over China. The iconic creature is a prominent feature of many festivals and celebrations, with many celebrants wearing brightly-colored costumes and performing elaborate dances in honor of the auspicious creature and all that it represents. To this day, it is taboo in China to deface a statue or image of a dragon.

Tianlong

THE UNICORN

Unicorns are perhaps one of the most recognized mythical creatures in contemporary culture. The unicorn has a complex and often contradictory history of symbolism, and was used in heraldry, alchemy, allegories, and appeared in legends dating back to the 4th century BC. The Greeks believed that unicorns were real animals, and gave many accounts of them in their compilations of natural history. There is some evidence that the first accounts of unicorns may have been from garbled descriptions of rhinoceros, and certainly in the 14th century there is an account of Marco Polo having seen what he believed was a unicorn, but by his account is unmistakably a rhino.

Generally depicted as a white, horse-like creature with a single spiraling horn in the middle of its forehead, the unicorn is associated with purity, chastity, faith, and honor. The unicorn is one of the few mythical beasts that is unmistakably good and pure, and was adopted by the Catholic Church as a symbol of Christ. It was said that the only way to capture a unicorn was to have a virgin maiden approach the beast, since the maiden's purity was the only thing that would calm the feral creature. Unicorns were accepted as rare and reclusive, and their horns were believed to have any number of magical healing properties, most notably the ability to neutralize poison and purify water.

The magical properties of a unicorn horn drove many people to search for these elusive creatures and inspired a lot of fakes. One of the most common substitutions was the horn of a narwhal, a type of toothed whale that lives in arctic waters, which has a long, straight, spiraled tusk that grows from its upper jaw. The popularity of these whale tusks allowed Vikings and sailors to sell them at many times their weight in gold. Other substitutions were made of powdered bone, rhinoceros horns, and the tusks of various animals, from elephants to warthogs.

Unicorn

THE VAMPIRE

The term "vampire" was not in common usage until the 18th century, but there is evidence in many cultures that blood-sucking corpse-like fiends have been around since prehistoric times. Early vampire-like creatures were often demons or evil spirits, and went by a variety of different names. Most of the earliest examples of blood sucking demons were pretty hideous. Usually they stank like rotten flesh, or looked like bloated rotting corpses or walking skeletal beasts.

The modern concept of a beautiful, seductive vampire came about in the 19th century when writers like John Polidori and later Brahm Stoker took the old legends and made them more exotic and scintillating. According to the modern version, vampires are the animated corpses of the dead. They are usually very beautiful or mysterious looking, and very charming. Vampires often have mind control powers or the ability to hypnotize people with their gaze. They are usually super-strong and supernaturally fast. A lot of stories hold that vampires must sleep in coffins or on dirt from their native soil. They can only be killed by driving wooden stakes through their hearts, and sometimes the stake must be made of a certain kind of wood. They are also susceptible to silver, they cannot bear the sight of crosses, and they cannot go out in the sunlight. Though modern authors have selected and discarded many of these rules, the things that make a vampire stand out are generally that they are basically immortal, drink blood to live, and have an aversion to sunlight. Originally considered evil beings, modern interpretations have vampires as all sorts of characters: good, ambiguous, or evil.

Vampires can make more vampires in a variety of ways, depending on the lore, but the most common version is by draining their victims and then feeding them their own blood. Historically, vampires could be created by a restless spirit that wasn't properly buried, they could be a regular person who was cursed from birth, or they could have just been bitten by a vampire. In some lore, vampires could take the form of bats, rats, wolves, and mist. Contemporary vampires hold so much fascination for our imaginations that vampires feature in TV shows, movies, books, and games.

Vampyre

THE WEREWOLF

Stories of humans that can transform into beasts can be traced to prehistoric times. It is believed that early shamanistic practices of wearing an animal skin to take on the powers or attributes of the animal may have inspired later legends of shape-shifting humans. In areas where there are no wolves, tigers, lions, and other animals are common were-creatures.

Werewolves, like vampires, have gained an enormous amount of popularity in more recent times, and many of the original folklore has been discarded in favor of more modern adaptations. What is generally agreed upon is that werewolves are men who can transform all the way or partially into wolves or wolf-like monsters, and often this transformation has to do with the phases of the moon. In folklore throughout medieval Europe, a werewolf was usually created by either a curse or being bitten by another werewolf. Sometimes a werewolf in human form could be discovered by certain traits, like excessively shaggy brows or hairy hands. It was believed that if you cut a werewolf in its human form you would see fur under its skin. Werewolves, unlike vampires, were not considered susceptible to holy objects or the sun.

Generally, to cure a werewolf, you had a few options. Sometimes you could steal and destroy the wolf skin, if you could find it (if it was the type of werewolf to take off its skin). Sometimes a tincture made of the herb wolf's bane would cure lycanthropy, or an exorcism. In Danish lore, simply scolding a werewolf could shame the beast out of the man. It was not until modern times that the idea of silver being used against werewolves came about. Werewolves were not always evil creatures, but usually they were dangerous and deadly pests, and often they were unable to control their bestial natures. The unlucky few who were cursed often committed acts of atrocity while transformed that they were doomed to remember with horror and shame while they were human.

Werewolf

THE XANA

The xana are a sort of water nymph common to Asturian mythology. They are almost always beautiful women, often with long, flowing blond hair and enchanting voices, who inhabit streams and caves in secluded places. In some legends, the xana are unfortunate young women who have been cursed, and often a young hero falls in love with them and must complete a series of tasks to break the spell on her. In other tales, the xana are magical beings that may be benevolent or evil according to their own whims. They often guard treasure, but in the legends that surround them, they rarely end up sharing that treasure, instead using it to lure the unlucky to their deaths.

The xana have a lot of similarities to certain fae creatures in English and Welsh legends. They can bear children, but often cannot raise them, so they will try to swap their own child with a human baby so that the human mother can nurse and raise their offspring. Sometimes in these tales, the xana can enter a home through a keyhole. Good xana will often become enamored of a hero for their purity or honor, and will help them or give them magical items. Often, xana will punish wicked people with as much zeal as they will help the good.

The fickle nature of these nymphs makes them dangerous and unpredictable. Generally, if they aren't the kind of xana that are actually unfortunate maidens under a spell, then they are a "traveler beware" kind of monster...as likely to drown you as they are to bestow gifts.

Xana

The Yeti

The yeti is reported to be a humanoid creature that inhabits the Himalayan Mountains in Tibet and Nepal. The yeti, also known as the "Abominable Snowman", may have existed in local folklore for a long time, but has a documentable history that dates back only to the late 1800's. The term "abominable snowman" actually comes from a mistranslation of the Tibetan word which means "rock-bear." Yeti are generally described as hairy beasts that walk on two legs. They gained popularity in the late 1800's when a bunch of European mountain climbers and explorers encountered various tracks, long distance sightings, and other evidence as they scaled the mountains.

Most accounts of yeti are inconclusive at best, but the legends of this reclusive snowy beast are persistent. There is no evidence that the yeti is a malicious creature, in fact it seems to be extremely shy. Most of the sightings of the creature have been at a distance, and although one explorer claimed to have actually killed one, it's likely he actually killed an endangered species of Himalayan bear. All of the reported tracks and sightings to date have eventually been attributed to bear or mountain goats, but the mystery of the elusive snowman remains. Eyewitness accounts and local legends insist that a mysterious bipedal ape-man lives somewhere in the inhospitable Himalayan Mountains!

Yeti

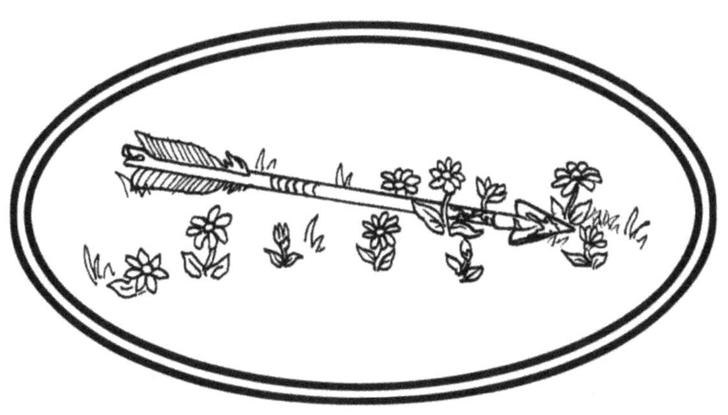

THE ZLATAROG

The story of the zlatorog had a long oral history in Slovenia before it was written down in 1868 by Karl Deschmann. The zlatarog is a mythical white deer, a chamois buck with beautiful golden horns. It was said to roam the valley of Triglav when it was a beautiful garden, and it kept the company of the White Ladies, who were good faeries. Together, these characters were very benevolent and often helped people who need them.

Everything was peaceful for the zlatarog until a young hunter was convinced to try to kill the magical deer. The zlatarog's horns were supposed to unlock a fabulous treasure kept under the mountain, and the young hunter was told that if he didn't gain this treasure he would never win the hand of his beloved. So the young man came upon the zlatorog and shot it, gravely wounding it. As the deer's blood spilled onto the snowy ground, the snow melted and magical red flowers sprang up. The zlatorog quickly ate some of these flowers and was immediately restored to health. He rushed at the young hunter, who was blinded by the light glaring off the deer's golden horns, and lost his footing on the perilous rocky mountain. The hunter fell to his death, and the zlatarog and the White Ladies left the valley, leaving it a desolate, rocky place.

In the spring, the hunter's young lover found his body in the river, and wept that her family's greed had driven him to his death, leaving the valley without its former protectors.

Zlatorog

About the Artist

FELIX EDDY grew up on an old farmstead outside of Buffalo, New York, with her parents, brother, lots of barn cats, a few dogs, and the occasional chicken. She took private painting lessons from a young age, but was drawing constantly on her own from the time she could hold a crayon.

Forever excited about history and mythology, Felix is a member of the Society for Creative Anachronism, and takes part in a number of other groups and conventions all over the country. She is currently enamored of several aesthetic movements, including Pop Surrealism and assorted "Steampunk" phenomena. The artists she admires most include such illustrious characters as Edward Gorey, Leonore Fini, Remedios Varo, Joseph Cornell, Gustave Dore, and Alfonse Mucha.

Felix attended Alfred University for Fine Arts, where she graduated at the top of her class in 2002. She moved to Binghamton a few years later, where she met a lot of artistic people and started showing her work and attending festivals. She currently resides in Endicott, New York, with more cats and some great friends and family.

Felix is a professional artist who is constantly creating and producing new works. You can see her latest artwork, check her upcoming exhibitions, order prints, or discuss commissions with her through her website at www.felixeddy.com. She also offers prints and posters of each of the creatures in this book. You can contact her through her website, or at felixxkatt@yahoo.com.

ACKNOWLEDGMENTS

This book would not have been possible without the love and support of my friends and family.

First and foremost, a big thank you to my parents, who have always been there to encourage me to do bigger and better things. They've managed to be there to help me in the best and worst of times, and I know I will never be able to thank them enough.

Thanks to Deanna, who has been there to talk me through some stupid ideas and into better ones, and encourage me when I was getting off-track. She's seen this book through from the beginning. She was there watching the booth at the art festivals and helping me look up obscure mythical beasts from her cell phone as I scribbled away.

A big thank-you to my brother, Pat, who has been helping me to run my household while my head was buried in books, research, nonsense, and art things.

Thank you to all of my friends, who read sections or oversaw my sketching processes, and offered suggestions and encouragement as I worked. Thanks to those of you who proof-read sections and edited for me, too, especially Andrei Guruianu, who has come through like a superhero for me with all my questions, dilemmas, and emergencies.

Finally, I would like to sincerely thank all the people who have supported my art—emotionally or financially—over the past several years. All the folks who meet me at art shows and gush over my work, or who look me up online and drop me a note...you guys really make it worthwhile for me. Thank you!

BIBLIOGRAPHY

Allan, Tony. *The Mythic Bestiary: The Illustrated Guide to the World's Most Fantastical Creatures*. London: Duncan Baird Publishers, Ltd. 2008.

Graves, Robert. *The Greek Myths*. London: The Folio Society, 1996.

Matthews, John and Caitlin. *The Element Encyclopedia of Magical Creatures*. London: Harper Element, 2005.

Pliny the Elder, trans. & ed by John Healy. *Natural History: A Selection*. Harmondsworth, Middx: Penguin, 1991.

Roob, Alexander. *Alchemy & Mysticism*. London: Taschen, 2005.

Rosen, Brenda. *The Mythical Creatures Bible: The Definitive Guide to Legendary Beings*. New York: Sterling Publishing Company, 2009.

Wikipedia. The Free Online Encyclopedia. Started in 2001. http://en.wikipedia.org/wiki/Main_Page.

(note... I scoured Wikipedia for information, but I did not keep track of every page I visited. This is an excellent place to start looking for information about obscure creatures and mythology).

If you liked this book, you may like some of our other titles.

To learn more about our authors and our current projects visit:
www.mirrorworldpublishing.com or follow @MirrorWorldPub
or like us at www.facebook.com/mirrorworldpublishing

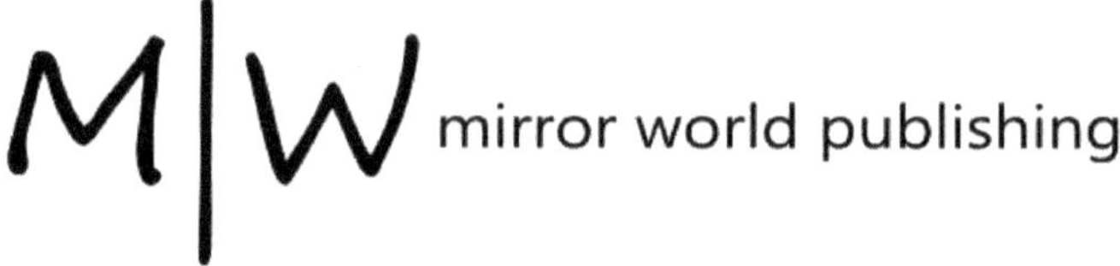

We appreciate every like, tweet, facebook post and review and
we love to hear from you. Please consider leaving us a review
online or sending your thoughts and comments to
info@mirrorworldpublishing.com

Thank you.